P9-DWH-815

Dear Parent:
Your child's love of reading starts here!

Every child learns to read in a different way and at his or her own speed. Some go back and forth between reading levels and read favorite books again and again. Others read through each level in order. You can help your young reader improve and become more confident by encouraging his or her own interests and abilities. From books your child reads with you to the first books he or she reads alone, there are I Can Read Books for every stage of reading:

SHARED READING
Basic language, word repetition, and whimsical illustrations, ideal for sharing with your emergent reader

BEGINNING READING
Short sentences, familiar words, and simple concepts for children eager to read on their own

READING WITH HELP
Engaging stories, longer sentences, and language play for developing readers

READING ALONE
Complex plots, challenging vocabulary, and high-interest topics for the independent reader

ADVANCED READING
Short paragraphs, chapters, and exciting themes for the perfect bridge to chapter books

I Can Read Books have introduced children to the joy of reading since 1957. Featuring award-winning authors and illustrators and a fabulous cast of beloved characters, I Can Read Books set the standard for beginning readers.

A lifetime of discovery begins with the magical words **"I Can Read!"**

Visit www.icanread.com for information
on enriching your child's reading experience.

I Can Read!™

SHARED READING

My First

WITHDRAWN

JUST A LITTLE SICK

BY MERCER MAYER

HARPER

An Imprint of HarperCollinsPublishers

To Diane, Bonnie, and Rita,
the elves

I Can Read Book® is a trademark of HarperCollins Publishers.

Little Critter: Just a Little Sick
Copyright © 2010 Mercer Mayer. All rights reserved. LITTLE CRITTER, MERCER MAYER'S LITTLE CRITTER and MERCER
MAYER'S LITTLE CRITTER and logo are registered trademarks of Orchard House Licensing Company. All rights reserved.
Manufactured in China.
No part of this book may be used or reproduced in any manner whatsoever without written permission except in the case of brief
quotations embodied in critical articles and reviews. For information address HarperCollins Children's Books, a division of
HarperCollins Publishers, 195 Broadway, New York, NY 10007.
www.icanread.com

Library of Congress catalog card number: 2009922327
ISBN 978-0-06-083556-9 (trade bdg.) —ISBN 978-0-06-083555-2 (pbk.)

Typography by Sean Boggs
17   SCP   10 9 8 7 6 5
❖
First Edition

A Big Tuna Trading Company, LLC/J. R. Sansevere Book
www.littlecritter.com

I am just a little sick today.
Mom says, "No school.
You need to stay in bed."

Being just a little sick
is fun.

I get breakfast in bed. Yay!

It is just plain toast. Yuck!

"I want Fruity Nut Crunch,"
I say.

Mom says, "You are too sick.
Go back to bed."

"I am not too sick
to play video games."

"Yes, you are," says Mom.
"Now go to bed and rest."

I am not too sick
to fly to the moon
on my rocket ship.

"The rocket ship ran out
of gas," Mom says.
"It needs to rest."

I am not too sick
to build a tent on my bed.
I am hiding from my bear.

Suddenly I don't feel good.

My bear and I go to find Mom.

Mom sends me back to bed.
She takes my temperature.

"You have a fever," says Mom.

I say, "I am sleepy."

I wake up from my nap.
I feel great!

I get dressed.

I will go out to play.

Mom says, "Oh, good,
you are all dressed.
Let's go to the doctor."

"But I am not sick anymore,"
I say.

Mom takes me to the doctor
anyway.

We wait and wait.

I put on a funny-looking robe.

The back is open.

The doctor checks my throat,
my nose, and my ears.

The doctor gives Mom something
to make me feel better.

We go home.
I can't wait to go out
and play with my friends.

"Oh, no," says Mom.
"The doctor said
you have to rest all day."

I am tired of resting!
I ask, "Can I please go
to school tomorrow?"

I changed my mind.
Being just a little sick
is no fun.

CONTRA COSTA COUNTY LIBRARY

31901062639853